TRAPPED

BY JAMES MOLONEY

ILLUSTRATED BY SHAUN TAN
COVER ILLUSTRATION BY SERG SOULEIMAN

Librarian Reviewer
Marci Peschke
Librarian, Dallas Independent School District
MA Education Reading Specialist, Stephen F. Austin State University
Learning Resources Endorsement, Texas Women's University

Reading Consultant
Elizabeth Stedem
Educator/Consultant, Colorado Springs, CO
MA in Elementary Education, University of Denver, CO

STONE ARCH BOOKS
Minneapolis   San Diego

First published in the United States in 2008
by Stone Arch Books
151 Good Counsel Drive, P.O. Box 669
Mankato, Minnesota 56002
www.stonearchbooks.com

First published in Australia in 1996 by Lothian Books
(now Hachette Livre Australia Pty Ltd)

Published in arrangement with Hachette Livre Australia.

Library of Congress Cataloging-in-Publication Data
Moloney, James, 1954–

    [Pipe]

    Trapped / by James Moloney; illustrated by Shaun Tan.

    p. cm. — (Shade Books)

    Summary: David and his parents move to a new town with a
huge storm drain that would be perfect for skateboarding, and in
spite of hearing warnings about a terrible accident that occurred
there, David is determined to try it out.

    ISBN-13: 978-1-59889-863-7 (library binding)

    ISBN-10: 1-59889-863-9 (library binding)

    ISBN-13: 978-1-59889-919-1 (paperback)

    ISBN-10: 1-59889-919-8 (paperback)

    [1. Skateboarding—Fiction. 2. Ghosts—Fiction.] I. Tan,
Shaun, ill. II. Title.
PZ7.M7353Tr 2008
[Fic]—dc22   2007004117

Art Director: Heather Kindseth
Graphic Designer: Kay Fraser

1 2 3 4 5 6 12 11 10 09 08 07

Printed in the United States of America.

TABLE OF CONTENTS

CHAPTER 1

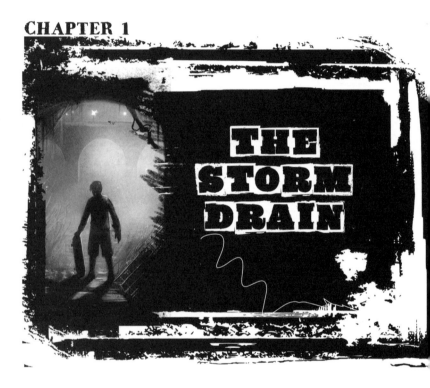

THE STORM DRAIN

I'm sure now that I saw him in the mouth of the pipe as we drove across the bridge. I could only see his legs sticking out. They were tempting me, inviting me to come down and look for him.

My parents and I were on our way home from the airport. We had just moved.

Our new town was a place I hadn't heard of until my father got a job there managing a big grocery store.

"Look, that's where I'll be working, David," Dad said, pointing out the window of the taxi.

I looked away.

I thought about the friends I'd left behind, thousands of miles away.

I wouldn't meet anyone new until school started in two weeks.

The taxi turned off the main road onto a bridge and I looked down.

I expected to see a creek or railroad tracks.

Instead, I saw a huge storm drain. It was about ten feet wide, and it looked like it was lined with concrete.

It was perfect for a skateboard. I sat up to get a better look.

That was when I saw him.

It was just a peek of legs and feet, but that peek was enough to hint that the legs and feet belonged to a boy my age.

He was waiting inside a huge pipe that stuck out from the gray wall of the drain.

Maybe it was my eyes playing tricks.

After all, I was thinking about my skateboard at that moment. I was happy that I'd slipped it into my suitcase instead of packing it deep inside one of our moving boxes.

I was sure that I had seen a skateboard resting against the boy's leg.

CHAPTER 2

AN ACCIDENT

Once we'd looked around the new house, there wasn't much to do.

Everything we owned was in a moving van, way back on the road somewhere.

Mom and Dad seemed restless.

I thought they'd like to talk without me listening to every word.

So I grabbed my skateboard and headed straight for that pipe.

I went inside it when I got there. The curved walls were covered with graffiti for the first fifty feet inside.

After that came darkness.

I was about to climb in and try out my board when a voice shouted, "Hey! You can't go in there!"

I saw three boys pushing their skateboards toward me.

"Why not? Plenty of kids have been in here. Look at all the graffiti," I shouted back, defending myself.

The three boys joined me near the pipe. Two of them stood like bodyguards around the boy in the middle. He seemed like he was their leader.

The one in the middle spoke. "You just can't." He paused.

He looked left and right, checking with his friends before he gave his reason. "Because of Simon and Justin."

My face must have shown that I didn't have a clue what he was talking about.

One of the other boys looked at his friends and said, "We've never seen this guy before. He's not from around here. Maybe he doesn't know."

The leader thought about this for a minute. His skin was tan and his face was sweaty.

I was sweaty too. It was so hot out.

"Is that right? You don't know about what happened?" he asked me.

I shook my head. "I just moved here," I said. They seemed to calm down after that.

The boy in the middle looked at me. "We used to skate in that pipe all the time," he said. "It was great."

The others nodded, staring into the darkness.

The leader said, "Last year there was an accident. Some of our friends got hurt. One kid especially. Now we're not supposed to go inside. The cops watch for us. They don't like us being down here."

Then they started to leave. They probably thought I would leave then, too.

But in the few seconds it took me to get on my board, I heard a noise from inside the pipe.

It was very quiet, but I knew right away what it was.

Way back in the pipe, someone was riding a skateboard.

CHAPTER 3

THE WET SEASON

The next morning I was still thinking about the sound I'd heard in the pipe.

How could anyone skate in the dark?

How could you ride by feel instead of by sight?

I knew that I had to find out.

When the moving van arrived just before lunch, I started looking through all of our boxes for Dad's flashlight.

The unpacking was slow, sweaty work.

To make it even more tiring, as the sun rose in the sky, the heat got worse and worse.

"This is the tropics, David," Dad explained. "The wet season is coming. Wait until the storms start. The rain doesn't just pour down. It floods!"

He spread his arms high and wide and wiggled his fingers dramatically as he lowered them. "You've seen that big storm drain at the bottom of the hill," he went on. "They say it can fill up in a matter of seconds."

Then I found the flashlight, so I stopped paying attention. I was out of there in a minute.

There was no sign of the boys down by the drain. A few people were crossing the bridge, heading toward the corner shop.

No one saw me when I climbed inside the pipe.

I had to duck my head and shoulders as I moved along. That made walking slow.

The sides of the pipe were cold and I shivered, and not just from the feel of the concrete against my shoulder. As the light dimmed, I found myself getting ready for the blackness ahead.

The farther I went, the more aware I became of sounds — my footsteps, my breathing. Every small sound seemed louder than normal.

I stopped and listened. The silence was scary. I wished there was some noise, any noise.

I decided that I had gone far enough. It was time to get on my board. But just as I did, I heard the squealing wheels of another skateboard.

What I had heard the day before was
true, then.

There was a boy riding his board inside
this pipe.

The thought that there was someone else
to share the darkness chased away my fear.

I switched on the flashlight and began
to explore.

"Hello!" I yelled. I heard my voice
crash along the pipe and bounce back at
me like a pack of dogs. The sounds of the
skateboard stopped and the darkness was
silent again.

I started walking, keeping the flashlight
pointed ahead of me and my board against
my leg. About fifty feet from the opening,
the pipe made its first bend, a long
gentle curve.

I forgot for a moment that there was someone else there. I only thought about the skill I would need to ride through this pipe by flashlight.

I would have to ride along the sides to stay balanced, looking ahead to avoid patches of slime under my wheels.

I searched for any other dangers. When the flashlight beam showed me some metal bars that stuck out from the top of the pipe above my head, I shined the beam on the roof, ignoring the ground altogether.

Out of the darkness at my feet, a voice whispered, "Justin? Is that you?"

CHAPTER 4

SIMON

I jumped back, shining the flashlight down to see who was there.

A boy lay stretched across the tunnel.

He wore shorts and sneakers, just like me. His T-shirt was ripped around the collar and was stretched out of shape. He didn't have a flashlight.

There was something else missing, too, but at first I wasn't sure what it was.

"You're not Justin," he whispered.

Then his voice changed. He sounded annoyed. "You're not supposed to be in here," he said. He scrambled to his feet as he spoke.

He was tall. He had to bend down more than I did. His greasy hair fell across his forehead and covered his eyes.

"Why didn't you warn me you were here?" I said. "You must have heard me yelling."

Then I realized what was missing. "Where's your skateboard?" I asked him.

Fear showed in the boy's eyes. He looked away. "They took it away," he said. "After the accident."

Even before he finished his sentence, I knew what he would say.

I had guessed who this kid was as soon as I recovered from the shock of finding him on the floor.

Now I was sure.

The boys I'd met the day before had mentioned an accident. I remembered the names they had said.

"You're Simon, aren't you?" I asked him.

He was startled. He paused before he replied, "How'd you know? I don't know you."

"I heard about you yesterday," I said.

"Are the other kids coming up here?" he asked. "They're not supposed to." He was shaking. He seemed scared stiff that the other boys might discover him.

"I heard another skateboard farther up the pipe," I said. "It's Justin, isn't it?"

I wasn't prepared for his reaction. If he denied it, to protect his friend, I would have understood.

If he relaxed a bit, and maybe smiled to try and make me part of the secret, that wouldn't have surprised me either.

Instead, he backed away from me again, into the darkness of the pipe. I never saw anyone look so sad.

"You heard it?" he whispered, as though he didn't want it to be true.

"Of course I heard it. Someone's up there riding a board," I said.

The boy turned back to me and I jumped.

His face seemed ready to explode with fear. His mouth hung open as if it was going to scream. His chin was shaking really hard, and his eyes were wide.

"It's Justin, isn't it?" I asked again.

"I don't know. Maybe it is," he said. He bent over and folded his arms across his stomach.

I realized that I'd been wrong.

When I first heard the story, I had imagined two boys climbing into the pipe, being careful to not be seen and excited by their daring.

Now I was starting to see a different picture. Two boys arguing. One wanted to take his board into the pipe and ignore the warnings. The other refused at first, then got worried and went in to find his friend.

"Why don't you go find him?" I asked. "Here, you can borrow my flashlight if you want."

His face turned even whiter. "No. No, I can't."

He looked up at the steel bars I'd seen earlier.

He seemed to be begging me to understand. "I can't go past here," he said. "I can't explain why."

Maybe he'd made a promise to himself. Maybe it was just plain fear. I didn't keep asking him about it. His fear was starting to spread to me.

There was silence until, finally, he said, "Would you go up there and look for him? Come back and tell me if you see him?"

"Me? No way. I'm not going past here either," I said, surprising myself.

I had been looking forward to going down the pipe, through the darkened curve with my flashlight lighting the way. Now I was afraid to go any farther.

"You wouldn't have to go far," he told me. "Just follow the noise until you see him."

"I don't know," I said.

"Please?" he asked quietly.

He was scared. If I said no, I'd be admitting that I was scared, too.

"It'll only take a few minutes," he went on. "Please, I need to know."

"Need to know what?" I asked.

"That it's Justin," he replied.

"Who else would it be?" I asked.

He didn't say another word. He didn't have to. The begging continued in his eyes.

I pointed the flashlight into the darkness ahead of me.

The inside of the tunnel became as bright as day. I could see clearly. I didn't have far to go. It wouldn't take that long.

"I'll just go a little ways and call out for him, okay?"

I heard myself say the words. Then I wished I could take them back.

Why did I say I'd do it?

CHAPTER 5

PUZZLE PIECES

I hadn't traveled very far when the pipe forked. I had to choose a direction.

It was not a hard choice. The branch on the right was the same size as the tunnel I was in. The left branch looked too small for a skateboard and rider.

My choice was made easier when the sound of a board echoed from the right. It stopped.

I called out, "Justin!"

There was no answer. He must have headed back up the pipe.

I didn't want to wait.

The farther I went, the more the pipe seemed to close around me, like I was being swallowed up in another world. I thought of the stories about people who'd been buried alive.

Questions clawed their way into my mind. How far below the ground was I? Where did this pipe go?

I thought about the boy I'd met. I was starting to think that Simon had been afraid of more than just the darkness.

What was it about this pipe that scared him and kept him from coming with me?

The place was starting to freak me out.

I decided to face it. I would convince myself that there was nothing to be scared of. My thumb was on the flashlight switch. I pressed it. The light went off.

It was a mistake. I'd never experienced total darkness like this.

Out in the open, at night, there were always the moon and stars, and I could always make out familiar objects like trees, a house, another human being. But not here.

I turned the flashlight back on, but the damage was already done. I had a new fear, that my flashlight might stop working. I would be lost in total darkness.

Simon or no Simon, I was going back. I turned around and took a few steps. Then the sound of a skateboard filled the tunnel. I couldn't tell how close it was.

The sound reminded me that I wasn't alone. At the same time, I felt angry. I was being teased, drawn into the pipe.

My anger turned me around again. I would find this Justin and bring him down to join his friend, no matter how far I had to go.

The pipe curved sharply, first one way, then the other. The slope became steeper in parts, and then leveled out. I counted the many smaller openings in the wall as I went.

Still, there was no sign of Justin.

I thought about the few minutes I'd spent with Simon. Mentioning the skateboard had scared him.

He'd been even more terrified when I told him I'd heard the sound, too.

Why should he be scared, if it was just his friend skateboarding?

Or was there something that Simon hadn't told me?

He seemed like he wanted me to see Justin. He'd mentioned it twice.

"Come back and tell me if you see him. Just follow the noise until you see him," he'd said.

My fear returned. I felt like I'd been sent along this pipe to see something, to catch a glimpse of something. Something that Simon couldn't believe was there.

What was so strange about Justin?

The boys who'd warned me about the pipe had talked about an accident. Two kids, Simon and Justin.

One of them had been badly hurt. That could mean anything.

They would have told me if one of the boys had been killed, right?

Now Simon's behavior began to fit with his words, like pieces of a puzzle.

The way he had sat in the pipe, just beyond the sunlight.

The way his face filled with terror when I appeared, a terror that went away as soon as he saw that I wasn't Justin.

Could it be true?

Could he have been waiting for his dead friend to appear out of the darkness?

I kept walking while these ideas took shape in my mind.

As the full horror spread through my body and my heart raced, I spotted something ahead.

As I came closer, my flashlight took away the darkness and I slowed down.

The pipe came to an end. It broke into four smaller sections. All of them were too narrow for a person.

I stood there, facing the dead ends.

I'd gone pretty deep into the dark tunnel, following a sound that was always ahead of me.

Where had the noise come from?

Who was making it?

I came up with an explanation that I didn't want to believe. I stood there, forcing myself to think.

Then a new sound filled the pipe. I forgot all about the possibility of ghosts.

CHAPTER 6

THE STORM

The pipe began to shake. I touched the cold concrete and felt the walls tremble under my hand.

This lasted three or four seconds. Then it went away.

I guessed what had caused the vibration. I remembered my father telling me about the rain here.

I moved closer to the four pipes with dead ends.

After ten seconds, there it was, the soft sounds echoing through the pipes.

Water. A storm had started up there, on the surface.

Before long, every drop would pour into these pipes.

I had to get out. Fast!

Crouching low, knees bent, I stepped onto the skateboard and kicked.

There was no time to experiment on the curved walls.

It wasn't fun at all. I just felt scared.

Light was my biggest problem. I couldn't see a thing.

I had to dodge patches of gravel and greasy streaks of slime.

I found myself shooting up the curved walls then back into the middle and up the other side.

When I'd gone a few hundred feet or so, I reached a really steep section.

The slope helped me to pick up speed and I thought I would make it without even getting wet.

As I hit a flat part, I flashed the light away from the floor directly in front and deep into the tunnel.

Right then, one of the wheels caught in a crack.

My board stopped. I didn't.

As falls go, I'd had worse. One time I had sprained my wrist. Another time, I twisted my ankle so badly that I couldn't walk on it for a week.

This time there was nothing broken, no bad cuts.

The problem was my flashlight. It was dead.

As I pushed the switch, I heard the tinkling of glass. The light was broken.

All around me, the pipe was pitch black. Thunder rolled through the tunnel.

I wondered if I was going to die.

CHAPTER 7

Without light, the skateboard was useless.

I could still walk to safety, but which way? I didn't know.

Over and over, I thought that I was going to die. I'd be like Justin, forced to ride a ghost skateboard through this pipe for the rest of time. My knees buckled and I collapsed onto the ground.

I listened for the sound of the water coming to drown me. Instead, I heard the shuffle of shoes on gravel.

Someone, or something, was coming along the pipe toward me.

The pipe curved in the direction of the footsteps. Slowly, a green glowing light began to appear on the wall. It got brighter as the crunching of the footsteps got louder.

Then he was in front of me. His body was glowing with the same weird green light. A skateboard was in his right hand.

As I backed away, the ghostly figure looked at me. "Come on," he said. "There's a storm coming." He saw my flashlight on the ground, surrounded by broken glass.

"Where's your board?" he asked. "You're going to need it."

Why was he so interested in my board? How did he know I had one in the first place?

Even though I was scared, I answered him. "It's back where I fell off it."

He stepped past me, found my board, and dropped it at my feet. "Follow me. Stay close," he said.

I froze.

What should I do? If I stayed there I was dead anyway.

I put one foot on my board.

The boy turned and pushed off ahead of me, holding a light out to the side so that we could both see.

He was a good skateboarder. Very good. Almost too good to be true.

Forget it, I told myself.

What did it matter if he was a green ghost? He was getting me out of the tunnel.

Ghost or no ghost, I had to trust him.

He called back for me to slow down. I thought we were about a hundred feet from the entrance.

I was going to make it. I was going to see daylight, and breathe fresh air.

Instead of going on, the boy stopped and picked up his board as though this was the end of the line.

"Why did we stop?" I asked, keeping my distance. Had he brought me this far just to trick me at the last minute?

He pointed to the side pipe that joined the main pipe. "This should have some water in it by now," he said.

When I looked down, I could see that the pipe was dry. "The water hasn't reached here yet, that's all," I told him. I just wanted to keep going.

"I don't know," he said. "Something is wrong."

We were so close to safety. The boy was confusing me, holding me back. "Take me the rest of the way. Please. Before it floods," I urged him.

"Wait," he said. "Believe me, something weird is happening. I've never seen this before."

Was he a ghost, keeping me stuck there when I could have been groping my way down the pipe in darkness?

Or was he a real kid who was trying to save my life?

"Are you Justin?" I asked. I held my breath, hoping that he'd say some other name.

"How did you know?" he asked.

Before I could answer, a sharp crack echoed down the smaller pipe, followed right away by the sound of rushing water.

I knew I'd been tricked. The boy had used my trust to lead me to where the force of the water would be the strongest.

There was no time to think. I had to get out of that pipe.

I slipped past him into the darkness, beyond the opening from the smaller pipe.

"No!" he shouted. "Don't!"

I went on, reaching out my arms to the side of the pipe to feel my way.

The boy grabbed my shirt, holding me. No matter how hard I tried, I couldn't break his grasp. Terror filled my mind.

I cried out, but instead of words I could only make grunts.

He was winning. He pulled me backward. The noise around us got louder. Any moment now the water would reach me.

The boy yanked me back into the larger pipe.

I was going to die.

CHAPTER 8

IT'S A
KILLER

A surge of water roared out of the pipe. Tumbling along at the front of it was a pile of garbage.

There were pieces of wood and metal, and other large chunks of debris.

It crashed into the main pipe below us like a tidal wave.

Justin released his grip on my arm.

"That stuff was junk that clogs the drain, like a dam. When the water built up behind it, it burst and came flying down the pipe all at once," he told me.

That made sense.

If I'd run away from him and gone into the main pipe, the full force of that wave of trash would have smashed into my back.

Justin had saved me.

I realized something else. Justin's hand had been warm and solid.

He was flesh and bone after all. He wasn't a ghost.

I didn't have much time to think. A new danger suddenly occurred to me.

"Now we're trapped," I shouted. "We can't get out through that. We'll be swept along. We'll drown!"

"No, we won't," he called back. "It's just a surge. It's the water that built up behind the trash. I'm going to get you out alive. Okay? Why don't you trust me?"

"Because I thought you were a ghost!" I shouted. The words were out before I could stop them.

"A ghost!" His laughter filled the pipe.

I said, "The light around you. It's green."

"It's a glowstick," he said. "Like for Halloween. It's a chemical light that glows for a few hours, then you throw it away." He held it out for me to see. "I got it from the store near the bridge when I saw you go into the pipe."

"You saw me?" I muttered. That answered another question, how he'd known I was in the pipe in the first place.

It all seemed obvious now. He must have come up the pipe after me and found Simon waiting for him.

I was about to say so when he called, "It's slowing down."

Within seconds, the water had died down to a trickle.

That was good, because the roar of water in the big pipe was getting closer fast.

Justin held up his hand to stop me. I saw that he looked scared for the first time.

He told me, "That water will get here in a few seconds. We have to ride out fast. Listen. Halfway down, on the last curve, there's a bar, about head height."

"Yes, I saw it," I said. "That's where I met . . ."

He cut me off, eager to get going. "That's where Simon and I crashed last year. Watch out, it's a killer," he said.

We set off on our boards, the green light in Justin's hand peeling back the darkness.

I followed him carefully.

We rode up on the walls. Then we slid down again, ready for the climb on the other side. It took all of my skills.

There was no room for ghosts. If I stuck to my board and kept up with Justin, I would live.

Nothing else mattered.

Justin crouched low and kept to the center of the pipe. I figured out that he was doing that because of the metal bar.

I bent down too, with my arms stretched out for balance.

Suddenly, there it was.

The bar looked deadly in the green glow.

Justin slid under it. Then I did.

We were clear. In seconds, we'd see daylight. Behind me, the roar of the water was closing in.

The last bend seemed endless. It looped around and around.

Finally, we were going straight. The light got brighter, and I could see a circle of daylight ahead.

I glanced over my shoulder and there it was. The wave.

No, it wouldn't get me now. The end of the pipe was too close.

I was flying before I had time to be afraid.

CHAPTER 9

THE TRUTH

I guess it only took a second to land. But when you're in the air, sure you'll crash and lose every piece of skin from your head to your ankles, a second seems to last forever.

Justin landed ahead of me, his wheels spinning. He'd made it. When I came down, the force of the impact jolted my ankles.

My board skipped, and then skidded. I fought with it, struggling for balance. With the control I had left, I pushed into a sideways skid to lose as much speed as possible. I fell anyway.

The skin on my hand burned. My knee burned, too.

Then I stopped moving.

The rain poured down on my face. I was soaked, but I was alive.

Justin stopped a few feet away and helped me up.

"Thanks for getting me out of there," I said.

He shrugged and smiled.

Looking up, we saw a group of boys gathered on the bridge. I recognized them as the same kids who'd warned me about the pipe.

They came down to the grassy bank above the drain.

"Please don't tell them what I said," I begged Justin. "About you being a ghost, I mean."

Justin laughed quietly. "Stop worrying," he said. "I'm not going to tell. It's not like you saw Simon up there. That would be something to tell them."

"What do you mean?" I asked.

He turned, ignoring the boys, who'd already reached the entrance to the drain. They'd be next to us in just a few seconds.

"I thought they told you," he said. "About the accident."

"What about the accident?" I asked.

He breathed in slowly. "Simon and I got caught by a storm, just like you," he explained. "But we weren't so lucky. We got washed down the pipe. You saw what it was like. I broke my arm, my leg, two ribs."

"What about Simon?" I whispered.

Justin said quietly, "Simon's shirt got caught on that bar in the last bend. He couldn't get free."

The pipe gushed water into the drain as Justin turned toward it. With his eyes on the wide pipe, he told me the truth at last.

He told me, "Simon drowned. He's been dead for more than a year."

ABOUT THE AUTHOR

James Moloney has worked at a fruit market and in a truck factory, but it was his experience as a young teacher in Australia that led to his early novels. His books have appeared regularly on lists for literary prizes and children's choice awards ever since. James and his wife, Kate, live in Brisbane, Australia, with their three children.

ABOUT THE ILLUSTRATOR

Shaun Tan was born in 1974 and grew up in Australia. Shaun began drawing and painting images for science fiction and horror stories in small-press magazines as a teenager. Since then he has received numerous awards for his picture books. He has recently worked for Blue Sky Studios and Pixar, providing concept artwork for forthcoming films.

GLOSSARY

behavior (bi-HAYV-yuhr)—the way someone acts

buckled (BUHK-uhld)—crumpled, gave way, collapsed

debris (duh-BREE)—scattered pieces of junk or broken things

forked (FORKD)—branched into two or more directions

graffiti (gruh-FEE-tee)—pictures drawn or words written on walls or other surfaces, usually illegally

obstacles (OB-stuh-kuhlz)—things that are in the way

surge (SURJ)—a sudden, strong rush or wave

tropics (TROP-iks)—a hot, rainy area

DISCUSSION QUESTIONS

1. When Simon asked David to look for Justin, he went farther into the pipe. What would you have done? Explain your answer.

2. Have you ever had a friend or classmate who died? What did you do to get over the sadness and grief that you felt? What advice would you give to someone in a similar situation?

3. Why did David ignore the boys who told him to stay out of the pipe? What would you have done?

WRITING PROMPTS

1. At the end of the book, David is talking to Justin and the other boys are about to reach them. What happens next? Does David tell them about Simon? Write another chapter!

2. Do you believe in ghosts or spirits? Write a story in which your main character meets a ghost.

3. David has just moved to a new city, and is happy to find somewhere to skateboard. If you moved, what things would you need? What places, stores, activities, or groups would you be happy to find?

TAKE A DEEP
BREATH AND

THE
DEADLY
DOLL

BY J. BURKE

▼▼ STONE ARCH *Fantasy*

*Caroline's family inherited a mysterious, old-fashioned doll.
Soon after it arrives, Caroline's mother becomes deathly
sick. Then the doll starts popping up in some very odd
places. Caroline thinks that the doll is out to get her mom.
Could a little doll be evil?*

STEP INTO THE SHADE!

Gavin is obsessed with hunting for treasure with his metal detector. He finds the perfect spot — a huge, sandy playground. Then he meets a bunch of kids who have a mysterious treasure hunt of their own. Gavin gets the feeling they want him to stay . . . forever.

INTERNET SITES

Do you want to know more about subjects related to this book? Or are you interested in learning about other topics? Then check out FactHound, a fun, easy way to find Internet sites.

Our investigative staff has already sniffed out great sites for you!

Here's how to use FactHound:

1. Visit *www.facthound.com*

2. Select your grade level.

3. To learn more about subjects related to this book, type in the book's ISBN number: **1598898639**.

4. Click the **Fetch It** button.

FactHound will fetch the best Internet sites for you!